TABULA RASA

SLEEPING DRAGONS BOOK 2

OPHELIA BELL

Tabula Rasa
Copyright © 2014 Ophelia Bell
Cover Art Designed by Dawné Dominique
Photograph Copyrights © Fotolio.com, DepositPhotos.com, CanStock.com

All rights reserved. No part of this book may be reproduced in any form or by any electronic means, including information storage and retrieval systems, without permission in writing from the author, except by a reviewer who may quote brief passages in review.

This is a work of fiction. Names, places, characters, and events are fictitious in every regard. Any similarities to actual events and persons, living or dead, is purely coincidental. Any trademarks, service marks, product names, or named features are assumed to be the property of their respective owners, and are used only for reference. There is no implied endorsement if any of these terms are used.

Published by Ophelia Bell
UNITED STATES

ISBN-13: 978-1544291567
ISBN-10: 1544291566

ALSO BY OPHELIA BELL

SLEEPING DRAGONS SERIES

Animus
Tabula Rasa
Gemini
Shadows
Nexus
Ascend

RISING DRAGONS SERIES

Night Fire
Breath of Destiny
Breath of Memory
Breath of Innocence
Breath of Desire
Breath of Love
Breath of Flame & Shadow
Breath of Fate
Sisters of Flame

IMMORTAL DRAGONS SERIES

Dragon Betrayed
Dragon Blues
Dragon Void

STANDALONE EROTIC TALES

After You
Out of the Cold

OPHELIA BELL TABOO

Burying His Desires

•

Blackmailing Benjamin
Betraying Benjamin
Belonging to Benjamin

•

Casey's Secrets
Casey's Discovery
Casey's Surrender

Waking up is hard.

CHAPTER ONE

In Camille's dreams, she was never the shy, bookish girl who got tongue-tied in the presence of a beautiful man. No, in her dreams she was the pursuer, dominant over her desires, the mistress of her own fantasies. The subject of those fantasies in recent weeks had been one man—lovely Eben—who had destroyed all her past fantasies in a single afternoon, just by being *him*.

While in the real world he barely spoke to her, in the dream realm he became her supplicant. There, he would kneel before her, begging for the honor of pleasuring her. Out of his mouth would spill the most deliciously dirty words. The power she held over him in the dark of night made her giddy with delight.

After hours working to translate the text etched around the jade throne in the ancient dragon temple, Camille had succumbed to exhaustion. She now dreamed she sat naked upon that very throne, flanked by the jade dragon statues. The setting was unlike past dreams, but the situation familiar enough for her fantasy to play out as it always did. Eben stood before her, naked. Her gaze traveled hungrily up his strong legs, over muscular thighs and narrow hips. His cock stood proudly erect and appeared massive to her inexperienced eyes, yet it didn't frighten her.

Camille's gaze lingered there, and she licked her lips, imagining the taste of the moisture that glistened like a tiny jewel clinging to his tip. Would he be salty or sweet? Still, there was so much more to him than his virile manhood. Her gaze moved higher, over his taut stomach, rippling with the evidence of a body well kept, over tight curves of pectorals and long, powerful arms dangling from wide, strong shoulders. So many moments had she caught herself staring at the way his muscles flexed when he would move—to lift his heavy trekking pack to his shoulders each morning. More recently, the image that came to mind was the bunching of his thick forearm when he stroked the column of the dragon statue's huge phallus the day before, when they'd first explored the room at the heart of the dragon temple.

Eben's face was what really incited her desire. The wide-set blue eyes that seemed to undress her on the rare occasions she managed to capture his attention, a perfect nose above his bow-shaped mouth—a mouth just made for doing those things he promised in her dreams.

Since the first day they'd met, two months earlier, her infatuation had grown with every stolen glance. While he rarely spoke to her, sometimes she would catch him looking, and each night her dreams would grow more intense until she woke in a sweat, her heart pounding and the flesh between her thighs craving contact.

But during her waking hours, she was far too reserved to follow through.

Words came more easily within the sanctuary of her subconscious. All she had to do was speak and he was kneeling at her feet.

"My sweet Eben. Tell me what you want to do to me."

He leaned forward and tilted his head to rest one rough cheek against her inner thigh, tickling her sensitive skin lightly with his short stubble. His gaze rested at her core, the intensity of his desire burning in his eyes, causing her own flesh to tingle and grow warm without a single caress.

The corner of his lips brushed her skin when he started speaking. "I want to kiss those pretty lips, so deep there can be no doubt how much I want you." His face tilted higher, gaze lingering on her plump, pink-tipped breasts. "I want to suck those perfect rosebuds until they're so hard and tender you beg me to fuck you."

With each word, he moved incrementally closer between her thighs, and now his lips barely brushed against her slick pussy. She had to fight the urge to tilt her hips closer to his mouth as the words gusted against her tender flesh. She held her breath, waiting, vibrating with desire in anticipation of what he would say next.

"And I want to bury my cock inside you so deep I touch your soul."

True to his word, Eben nestled his face in the cleft between her thighs, fastening his lips against her slick folds. The wet heat of his mouth always startled her at first, hotter even than the flesh he latched onto. But shortly she lost herself in the sensations. He plunged his tongue deep inside her, sliding it in and back out in a languid thrust. The licks grew slower and longer with each pass, slipping up higher and swirling around and around her clit that already throbbed thickly with arousal.

Each curling tease of his tongue sent little jolts of pleasure through her body, bringing her nearly to the edge before he stopped. She braced herself for the next step and wasn't disappointed. Rising higher on his knees, he latched on to one nipple, sucking until she gasped and arched her back. He worshiped the other in kind, swirling his tongue around her areola once before pulling the pink tip between his lips. When both nipples were thoroughly attended and aching from his attention, he took her face between his large hands, gazing deeply into her eyes.

"Take me in, baby. Let me fuck your tight, virgin pussy."

She spread her legs wider, inviting his thick shaft into her. The sharp pain of tearing flesh came first, followed by the exquisite pressure of him filling her. Her virginity was ever present, undeniable even in these nocturnal interludes, so she used it as an anchor. It made the dream seem all the more real.

It never took long after that. He would fuck her soundly, whispering all the most suggestive things he planned to do to her, and within a few minutes they would both be crying out each other's names while they came.

Camille would awaken, replete and glowing with satisfaction. She would spend the rest of the day in a happy buzz, not fazed in the least by the petty annoyances of their expedition, or even Eben's generally circumspect attitude toward her.

Except this dream changed. When they were at that cusp and her impending climax began to grip her, an unfamiliar voice spoke through Eben's lips, the words exuding a power that tickled inside her eardrums.

"It is not yet time, my flower. To have him you must awaken one of mine first. You must give your virgin gift to my brood to get your heart's desire."

She awakened with a frustrated groan. Not time yet? Then she remembered her revelation earlier that evening. The ritual would keep any human in the temple from finding sexual satisfaction unless they were offering it to a dragon. *What did they call it? Their Nirvana?*

Apparently the Queen had reprimanded her in her dreams just now. Camille wasn't sure if she should feel special or not, knowing they needed her in particular to ensure the ritual's completion.

Right now, she was just incredibly frustrated, her body tingling still with Eben's imagined touch. It may have been the lack of release, but she wanted him so badly she could taste it.

During their journey, she'd tried to come up with ways to seduce him. Each day she'd tried to find moments when he would be alone. She would start to go to him, just to talk, but always ended up paralyzed by indecision and anxiety over taking that first step. Still, she knew she wanted him to be her first.

The difficulty was compounded by the fact that he and Erika had slept together nearly every night of their trip and didn't do a whole lot in the way of disguising the fact.

But not every night, Camille reminded herself. *Not the night before we arrived here.* That gave her a shred of hope, as did the subtle looks she sometimes caught him throwing her way.

She would just have to find him. There was a ritual to carry out. A sex ritual if she'd interpreted the etchings around the throne correctly. She imagined convincing him to assist with her part of it. *Help me find a dragon to*— To what? Give her virginity to? That thought brought her up short. If she were going to be part of the ritual, Eben wouldn't be her first after all. But to have him there with her, even just watching—the thought drove her back to the camp to find him.

But his sleeping bag was empty. As were Erika and Kris's. No! Tonight of all nights she needed him, and he was with *Erika* again?

"Camille?" Hallie's groggy voice spoke in the dim light. "Y'okay? W'assup sweetie?"

She realized she must've cursed out loud. "Nothing. Just burning some midnight oil to translate. Go back to sleep, Hal."

Her friend rolled back over in her sleeping bag. Camille felt a little guilty for not at least letting Hallie know what was going on. The other woman had been her closest friend in the group since Erika had brought them all together with the promise of adventure and academic renown. Hallie had even encouraged her to pursue Eben in spite of the obvious connection he and Erika had. *It's just a casual thing between those two, sweetie*, Hallie had said. *I see the way he looks at you.* Except now that Camille finally had the courage to chase him, she couldn't even find him.

The sleeping bodies of Dimitri and Corey didn't budge when she stole past them back into the corridor to search for Eben. She hoped he wasn't actually with Erika for once.

She navigated the darkened reaches of the maze that was the underground compound they had discovered. None of the multitude of intricately carved jade doors that lined the corridor walls gave entry. She tried them all until she finally came back to the beginning, frustrated. She stared at the huge, dark door that led to the passage behind the throne where the five doors of the ritual were concealed. Eben wouldn't have gone to those doors first, would he? He couldn't know about the ritual. But if Erika had found him, perhaps…perhaps they'd already begun.

Her chest tightened with rage and hurt. To think he was embarking on the beginning of this ritual with Erika and not with her—even if he and Erika weren't in love—somehow made their relationship something beyond Camille's reach. What if he'd left her behind without a backward glance?

"Dammit!" She angrily wiped a stray tear from her eye. Hoping she was mistaken, she pushed through the heavy door and quietly slipped into the shadows of the corridor beyond. Within several yards, the light from an open doorway spilled out across the pale stone of the floor before her. The most startling thing was the series of sounds that accompanied it. A chorus of urgent noises met her ears—the moans and whispers of people in the throes of ecstasy.

Consumed equally by jealousy and eager curiosity, she crept closer, keeping to the shadows just outside the door. She paused, hidden behind one of the large guardian statues that flanked all the doorways in this place. The carved white dragon kept her concealed and still gave her a perfect vantage to see everything happening in the room.

She stifled a gasp at the sight that was both disturbing and arousing. Erika was on her hands and knees on a low altar.

Behind her crouched a large creature the likes of which Camille had only seen in storybooks, its red scales glimmering like translucent jewels in the glowing lights. Long, red claws delicately gripped Erika's naked hips as it plunged its thick, smooth penis in and out of her. His cock looked so big he had to be uncomfortable for Erika, but she writhed and moaned and pushed back against the dragon's cock with obvious, enthusiastic enjoyment. Camille couldn't pull her eyes away from the sight. Heat coalesced between Camille's thighs while she watched, throbbing in time with every thrust.

After a moment, the dragon's wings extended, blocking Camille's view of everything but where his hips were joined with Erika's, and he bucked against the woman's ass as he climaxed with a low, velvety roar.

Camille thought her eyes were deceiving her when the dragon shimmered and shrank down to the size and shape of a large man, pulling Erika back into a tender embrace and nuzzling soft words Camille couldn't hear. She was comforted by the fact that the large red-haired man was decidedly not Eben, but where was Eben?

A motion at the far end of the room caught her eye. She drew her hand to her mouth to suppress a cry of astonishment. In an almost perfect reflection of her dream, Eben knelt, naked, between the thighs of a rigid statue of a beautiful woman. The figure was so much more than a woman, though. She had shimmering lavender skin that hinted at a scaled texture and majestic horns extending from her forehead, coiling back behind her. Sprouting from her back like sails were a pair massive wings.

Before Camille's eyes, the lavender dragon-woman shimmered as though the light had changed, but there had been no shift in the ambient lights of the room. Camille heard Eben groan as he latched his lips onto one bare, stone breast. In the most surreal of motions, his hips seemed to sink against the statue like he'd just shoved his cock in deep. Camille's pussy clenched and she groaned in empathetic ecstasy, wishing so hard that she were the object of his attention just now.

Her skin prickled beneath her clothing while she watched. Too hot…it was too hot in this dark corridor. She closed her eyes and rested her cheek against the cooler stone of the statue she hid behind. The sounds of passion that rolled over her only made her temperature rise.

She swiped a hand over her sweat-drenched neck and down her chest, gasping when her palm brushed over her breast, causing one nipple to stand erect. Experimentally she teased the other nipple and her eyes fluttered closed in response to the pleasant tingle that resulted.

She opened her eyes again to see Eben's head still bent to the statue's breast, sucking on the dark purple jade of its nipple. She shoved her tank top up and tweaked her own nipples trying to mimic what it might feel like to have his tongue on her. Oh God, her head spun with the pleasure of it. Stronger heat tingled between her thighs, but she knew it wasn't sweat making her wet down there.

She hastily stripped off her tank top and pressed her bare breasts against the silky smooth jade of the statue in an effort to cool herself off. The cool stone rubbed pleasantly against her nipples, relieving more of her tension but leaving behind a deeper need.

Eben let out a surprised grunt. He glanced between himself and the statue of the dragon-woman who now glowed with a subtle light that emanated from deep within, growing stronger with each thrust of Eben's cock. His hand disappeared between them and Camille could see his shoulder flexing with the hidden motions of his hand between the dragon-woman's thighs.

The visuals that image incited were too much for her to bear. She was beyond modesty now. It was just her and the silent statue of the guardian in front of her. She unzipped her shorts and slipped a hand into her panties. The fabric was sticky wet from her arousal, and her pussy tingled in anticipation of her touch.

She leaned against the statue and braced one knee on its heavy, smooth thigh, spreading herself open. Oh, she'd never been so wet before. Her clit had never felt so much like a swollen bundle of nerves, ready to burst with a single touch. She believed she could have come with the slightest pressure just then, but knew it couldn't happen. Not after the ending of her dream. *You must awaken one of mine,* the voice resounded in her head, and for the first time she was feverish enough to want to make it happen. But how?

She clenched her eyes in frustration, suppressing all the worst curse words she could think of but would never actually say out loud. When she opened her eyes, the remedy to her need stood proudly before her in the form of the polished white jade cock that jutted up between the guardian dragon's thighs.

All the guardian dragons were posed identically, like loyal dogs, resting back on their haunches, arms upraised and wings unfurled. If it weren't for the presence of their large phalluses, they'd have made comfortable seats with their thighs perfectly parallel to the ground and their arms outstretched above them. It occurred to her perhaps they were meant to serve a different purpose. *Her* purpose.

She stood, now practically within the embrace of this guardian, and the feel of its polished skin against hers suddenly felt a lot more intimate than it had a moment earlier. Her face flushed savagely. He could be alive, she remembered, and here she'd been wantonly rubbing her body all over him. But that's precisely what she should be doing, wasn't it?

She gripped the base of the dragon statue's erection to test it. Her hand didn't quite close around its girth, but it was smooth and soft, polished to a high shine and perfectly proportionate to what she'd always imagined Eben might look and feel like, only much, much bigger—so big she was a little terrified.

With a fascinated gaze, she let her hand slide slowly up the shaft to the tapered tip, then back down. Her palm tingled the entire length of him. He was a little warm, particularly at the base, though the smooth, twin globes of his testicles were cooler to her hot touch. The smoothness of him encouraged her to stroke again and wonder if Eben had the same texture or if he would be softer, more pliant, and would he have a slight curve, too.

She glanced quickly into the room again. The sights inside caused another surge of heat to rise between her thighs. Erika now rested astride the red-maned man, and Eben's pretty, lavender dragon had fully awoken. She was riding him as he sat on the bench, his hands tightly clenching her ass while he plunged his cock into her.

Camille pushed her shorts down over her hips and stepped out of them, eying the penis of her statue with some trepidation. Was she crazy to try this? What would Eben or the others think if they knew? Then Eben's murmurs from inside the room hit her ears.

"You like my hard cock deep inside your pussy, don't you baby?" The dragon-woman let out a hum of appreciation in response.

The sound of Eben's voice reminded Camille of her dream, and a violent flutter of need erupted deep in her belly, making her close her eyes and moan softly. When she opened them again she focused with determination on the statue in front of her.

"This is going to hurt," Camille said as though the dragon could hear her. Her voice shook a little, but she wanted this. She *needed* this. She climbed up onto his thighs and braced her hands on his shoulders.

Leaning forward slightly, she raised her hips and positioned herself above the head of the jade cock. Each brush of the stone against her skin, from her breasts against his chest to her slick folds against the solid tip of his cock, was enough to make her shudder with increased desire. When she pressed down, her lips spread wide and she pivoted her hips in a tight circle, sliding her clit around the tapered head. Little pulses of pleasure shot through her as she did so, making her moan softly.

"You feel nice." She looked into the dragon's stony eyes beneath his horned brow and imagined she could see a flicker of recognition there. "Are you ready for my virgin pussy to wake you up?" She giggled nervously at her attempt at dirty talk, but it somehow made things easier. Finally she angled her hips so that his tip pressed directly against her hot, clenching opening and began to press down slowly.

She stopped when she hit painful resistance. *Pretend you're ripping off a Band-Aid, silly. Just get it done.*

With that thought, she gritted her teeth and plunged her hips downward, seating herself entirely onto the dragon's massive erection with a loud cry. She immediately bit her lip and blinked away the tears that sprung to her eyes in response to the sting of her hymen breaking and the thick shaft stretching her wide open. She glanced into the room, but the others were being far too uninhibited in their own fun to have heard her little outburst.

In an attempt to distract herself from the pain, she leaned against the dragon's chest and grazed her nipples over the smooth stone again. At the same time, she began rubbing her clit gently with one finger, the zing of pleasure making the ache in her pussy all but disappear. Bracing her knees on the statue's thighs, she rose up slowly, her eyes fluttering at the slick friction of the smooth polished cock as all its contours rubbed against her sensitive inner flesh. She could even feel the thick ridge on the underside that led to the rounded flare of its head.

"Oh, wow, you do feel good," she murmured, sinking back down again. The pressure of the dragon's thick length inside her caused a pleasant buzz of sensation with each stroke, up then back down, as slowly as she could.

After the third stroke the pain was completely forgotten, replaced by urgent need to find her peak. She sensed that this time when she came it would be nothing like the times she'd toyed with herself to orgasm. No, she was filled so completely by the hard, smooth stone, she almost forgot she was fucking an inanimate object.

A fresh sheen of sweat broke out over her entire body and she panted out little whimpers against the dragon's chest. The temperature beneath her palms seemed to rise with each thrust of her hips. The cock deep inside her had more give against her needful thrusts, but she had no frame of reference to consider why.

She turned her head to face the open doorway just visible beyond the edge of the dragon's wing that still shielded her from view. A shiver of pleasure ran through her at the sight of Eben, standing now, his beautiful cock erect and about to be serviced by the pretty dragon-woman on her knees before him. Oh, to taste him like that. Then her eyes flitted to Erika who now lay back, her chest arched up and her pussy being thoroughly attended to by the red-haired dragon-man with a tongue that looked impossibly long and agile.

"I wonder, do you have a tongue like that?" she whispered to her serene and silent lover. Impulsively she brushed her lips across the end of his carved and slightly open snout, teasing her tongue between the smooth jade of his lips. He tasted of earth and sex, and a tiny jolt hit her tongue like she'd just touched it to the end of a battery.

The sharp sensation set off a chain reaction through her body. The tingling began in her core and her pussy began to clench in steady spasms. It came on so suddenly it surprised her. She clutched at the dragon's shoulders, gasping for breath, but unable to stop moving her hips—it felt so good. Then it overtook her like a wildfire, consuming her from head to toe.

She arched her back and cried out, rising up and slamming down again and again just to prolong the pleasure. The dragon's shoulders gave beneath her fingertips and his wings shuddered. His eyes flashed bright silver; a gust of white smoke rushed from his mouth followed by a low, curious growl.

With his first solid thrust back, she screamed in unbridled ecstasy, and everything went black.

CHAPTER TWO

In spite of the spectacular blow job he was enjoying, Eben's attention immediately shifted to the sound of the scream from outside the door. He placed a hand against the dragon Issa's cheek, but she'd already slipped her sweet, violet lips off his cock and turned her head to face the direction of the noise.

"The virgin has awakened a guardian," she whispered, her eyes growing wide.

"What?" Eben asked. He looked toward the doorway. Erika and Geva were equally distracted by the sound, Geva already striding toward the door.

A second later the figure of a huge, muscular man filled the doorway. He had white hair flowing to his shoulders, interrupted by two huge horns that jutted up from his brow. Intense, silver eyes surveyed the room from beneath heavy, white eyebrows. He held the slack form of an unconscious, naked woman in his arms.

"What the fuck?" Eben muttered. Was he another dragon come to life? He must be, considering those horns and his unworldly eyes. When Eben spied the long, golden length of Camille's braid trailing over the man's arm, cold rage coursed through him. Before he could think, he was running for the man, ready to pummel him to pieces, no matter how much bigger he was.

"Let her go!" Heedless of his nakedness he swung a hard punch that squarely met the man's jaw. In spite of the strength behind the punch, it had no effect aside from numbing Eben's arm to the elbow.

"Eben, no!" Erika shrieked. Three sets of hands soon held him back.

"Eben," Issa's softer voice said. "Let him speak. She awakened him, he couldn't have forced her. The virgin always makes her own choice during the ritual, and she made hers. Much sooner than is common, but still, it was meant to happen." Looking at the towering dragon-man who held Camille's unconscious body she said gently, "Roka, is this the virgin?"

The large, pale man nodded his horned head solemnly but didn't speak.

Eben clenched his fists ready to swing again, but thought better of it. "She doesn't belong to you, you bastard," he bit out through clenched teeth. "What the fuck did you do to her?"

The pale eyes narrowed on him, assessing him and contemplating. He looked like he was about to speak but held his response in check.

"She chose you, didn't she, Roka?" Issa said, ignoring Eben's outburst. "That means you have unlimited leave to speak now."

The man studied Issa from beneath a creased brow. His lips pursed and his frown deepened. After a pregnant moment he took a breath. In a deep, growling voice he said, "Her nirvana awakened me, but she fell unconscious before the awakening was complete. I am worried for her."

He turned his gaze to Eben, his low voice steady and calm. "This woman has a mild affliction. If you care about her, human, you will let me heal her affliction. I will give her to you now as a show of trust until you decide."

Eben nodded and held out his arms. When the larger man transferred Camille to him, Eben immediately carried her to the altar in the center of the room and sat with her cradled in his lap.

"Cammy, wake up." He caressed her cheek, noting how flushed and warm she was to his touch. "Someone bring her some water!" he called out to the room. Unsure what else to do, he bent and whispered in her ear. "Camille, it's Eben. Please wake up, baby."

He gazed at her unconscious face, regretting that he'd never tried to talk to her in depth, to nurture some kind of connection. He'd been such a fool.

He wasn't oblivious to the way she'd looked at him since meeting her months ago, but had always preferred a woman to make the first move, something she never seemed too keen on doing. Over the course of their journey, he'd watched her covertly, curious to see if she would come out of her shell. When she finally did, it was only when she believed he wasn't looking. During those rare moments, he would catch her in uninhibited discussion with one of the others and marvel at how beautiful she was. Unfortunately she always clammed up as soon as she caught him watching. Her pretty blushes as a result had begun to incite a kind of desire even Erika had never been able to draw from him.

A couple weeks into their expedition he'd finally decided to do something about it, yet she'd somehow inadvertently turned the tables on him. He found himself at a complete loss as to how to approach her, yet wanted her more than ever.

The idea of her being with another man enraged him after all the nights he'd spent fantasizing about being with her.

He looked up when the large figure of Roka knelt in front of him. "Leave her alone!" he yelled, shooting the other man a heated glare.

Issa sat beside Eben and laid a gentle hand on his arm. "Eben, he can help, but you need to help him, too. The part of the ritual to awaken him is incomplete."

"He looks awake enough to me. He can go fuck himself."

Roka snorted. "If only it were that easy. But that's not how it works. She chose me; she awakened me with her nirvana. But if I don't find my own with her I will sleep again and the ritual is rendered null."

Erika piped up. "Null? You mean we'd have to start over?"

"Not entirely," Issa said. "But you would need a fresh virgin. If you have one it should be no issue, but either way Roka will sleep for another cycle for having failed in this one." She gave Roka a mournful look and traced her lavender fingertips over one of his horns.

Eben darted his eyes between the two dragons, trying to comprehend what they were saying. He turned and looked plaintively at Kris who still stood in the corner, every bit as much a sentinel as all the statues that littered this place. Kris only nodded slightly and said, "She speaks the truth."

The body in Eben's arms shifted and a soft, groggy voice said, "Eben?"

"Camille? Oh, thank fuck. Are you alright?"

"What's going on? Where am I? Did…did it work?"

He glanced at Roka, who now sat back on his haunches watching silently. Eben met the man's eyes and swallowed tightly before looking back down at Camille's pretty, flushed face. "If you mean did you manage to wake one of them, yes. I'm impressed." And, in truth, he was impressed. The knowledge that she'd taken it upon herself to do something so overtly sexual changed his perception of her drastically, and in a way that aroused him to no end.

"I did? Where…where is he?" she asked bashfully. Eben raised his eyes to Roka.

Camille turned her head. "What's your name?" she asked.

"Rokaurasaelaethessis. They call me Roka, my love."

She shifted and the slight movement reminded Eben how very naked and soft she was cradled in his arms.

"You can call me Camille. After all, we did just…um…*fuck*. If we're being super technical, I kind of raped you."

Roka nodded. "Yes, we did, Camille. And no, you didn't rape me. I was born willing, as are all dragons. But something happened to you before my awakening was completed. Are you alright? My only care is for your well-being."

Camille's eyes widened and she sat up abruptly in Eben's lap. It took all his concentration to focus on her words and not the insanely fantastic feel of her lush bottom against his swelling erection. Her complete lack of modesty under the circumstances surprised him, too.

"You didn't finish? Oh no! I remember what the text says. You have to finish! The ritual depends on it!"

Roka nodded and met Eben's eyes, the gesture indicating some deference to his feelings at least. Eben slid his hand possessively around Camille's waist, wanting nothing more than to touch her now, to lay her down and spread her open and have her, and damn the ritual. With the barest glance, Roka rose and walked away.

Eben grimaced at the pang of guilt he felt and called out. "How much time do you have before it's too late?"

"Once the ritual is begun it must be completed within the span of a day. I have only a few hours."

Would it be enough time for Eben to get used to the idea of watching Camille fuck this other man? He couldn't decide if he'd hate it or enjoy it.

Eben looked down at Camille again. Her brow was creased and she gnawed distractedly at her lower lip. He followed her gaze to where Erika was seated on a polished jade chaise along one wall, resting in intimate connection with Geva. The red dragon-man seemed to be telling her quiet stories while he caressed her from head to toe.

"Erika's done with me," he said. "I was never enough for her."

"Are you sad?" She looked into his eyes without judgment or accusation—only curiosity.

"No. I'm …Christ, Camille, ever since I met you I haven't been able to think of anything else. You're all I want. I just hope you want me, too."

Her eyes widened at his confession, and her mouth made a soft little O shape that just made him want to kiss her. She shot another look at Erika. "But…all those nights? I mean, Erika's so much more…experienced. How could I measure up to her?"

"I'm not exactly a delicate kind of man, you know, but I'd love to help you *be* experienced."

She shifted around to straddle his legs, completely shameless about how very naked they both were. This new version of her dazed him. She gripped his jaw in both hands and kissed him, long and slow, and so sweetly. She was a study in contradiction now, kissing him like that after having done something incredibly erotic that he wished like hell he could have witnessed, and apparently willing to do even more with the dragon she'd awakened. The thought of getting to see her in action again decided the issue for him. It made his cock throb in anticipation.

"Oh, Eben, I want it all. I want to be *dirty*. Consider me a blank slate just waiting for you to teach me everything."

He held her closer, reveling in the way her curves pressed against him in all the right places. She tilted her head with a sigh when he nuzzled at her neck.

"Do you mean everything?" he murmured against her skin. "Because there's another man over there who you left hanging." Eben raised his eyes to look past her. Roka still waited on a bench across the room, watching them with an expression of overt desire.

She followed his gaze and whispered, "Do you mean…*both of you?*"

He only quirked a corner of his mouth suggestively, and noted that Roka had to have heard her based on the other man's body tensing and his eyes flashing expectantly.

A bright flush rose up Camille's chest and colored her cheeks. The way her breathing seemed to quicken made him wonder if all that blushing during their expedition hadn't been out of shyness after all. Maybe it was because she'd been turned on whenever she looked at him.

"You're excited about getting to fuck him again, aren't you?"

She clenched her eyes shut and after a second nodded. "How…how does this work, with two of you?"

Eben shrugged slightly, imagining all the potential configurations. "We'll just have to see what happens. I want you to myself for a few minutes first, if that's alright?"

CHAPTER THREE

Camille relaxed in Eben's arms when he lowered his head and kissed her. Oh how delicious his kiss tasted, better than she had imagined. His tongue teased and caressed, prodding deeper, then pulling back. His hand grazed over her hip and up her side to cup her bare breast. The electric sensation of his thumb against her nipple made her inhale sharply.

He laughed. "I love seeing you turned on like this. Fuck, you're beautiful." His hand pulled back and hovered over her skin, but it was the look in his eyes that made her quiver before he touched her again. His eyes intently followed his caress upon the curve of her breast. He traced the underside, skimmed across to her other breast and up over the top, seemingly mesmerized by both pale mounds. With a bolder motion, he skimmed around again, but brushed her nipples on the second pass. The brief contact made her clit twinge and her heart speed up.

"Oh? Why did you never tell me so before?" she murmured, sliding her palms over his shoulder, rejoicing in the feel of him tight against her and apparently in no hurry to let her go. As eager as she was to move things along, she was enjoying his caresses too much to rush.

"I always thought it," he said, apparently distracted by the texture of her nipple against his palm. "I imagined your face while Erika fucked me most nights. She was good, but never as perfect as you."

She gaped at him. "You thought of me when you were… with her?" she asked, slipping her fingertips up into the hair at the base of his skull and beginning to pant a little in response to his touch.

If she weren't so astounded she'd have thought the flush that rose up to color his cheeks was cute. But this was a revelation.

"Camille…I told you I've wanted you since the first time I saw you. I meant it. That first day in that bar in Boston. I probably seemed rude, but I couldn't stand up because I had such a hard-on after you walked through the door." As if to agree with his point, his hard cock twitched perceptibly between them.

"But…why? Why didn't you ever tell me?" she asked. Confusion tangled within her stomach. All those nights fantasizing about being with him, having to listen to him with someone else through the thin fabric of their tents. She was torn between wanting to punch him and drag him down to the floor, begging him to make love to her.

His brow creased above his closed eyelids and he seemed hesitant to meet her gaze again. He shook his head a tiny bit and let out a little sigh. "I misunderstood you, I guess. At first I figured you were just too shy. Boy did you prove me wrong. You just climbed right on that dragon cock didn't you?" He opened his eyes and gave her a challenging smirk.

She punched him softly. "Yeah, but this place…there's something…" *Magical*, she thought, but her logical mind rebelled against articulating it. As if somehow it made more sense for her physical need to overwhelm her to the degree that she'd pleasure herself on a statue. Who then *magically* came to life? Who was she kidding? Knowing what all the text etched in the floor around the throne meant didn't make it any easier to grasp.

"Something in the air that makes you horny as shit. I know."

She nodded, grateful that Eben seemed to have the same mental block. "Yes! Exactly. And I was so turned on watching you with the purple dragon-lady. And Erika with the red one… wow, those two."

Eben chuckled. "Yeah, they were spectacular together."

"What about your dragon?" she asked, suddenly concerned about the dragon-woman who she'd summarily displaced. She hadn't seen the woman since regaining consciousness.

As if hearing her question the female dragon seemed to materialize beside them. "Hello, Camille. You may call me Issa. I'm free now, thanks to your lovely man." Issa ran her fingers through Eben's thick, blond hair and give him a sensuous kiss.

When she pulled back she smiled with pure, white teeth framed by a pair of luscious purple lips. "Don't fret on my account. Just promise me you'll treasure him. He is such a prize. Besides, I can't bear to part two lovers, so I've agreed to let Roka have you both. He will treat you well."

When she finished speaking, Issa bent and rested her lips against Camille's. A smooth, sweet tongue gently parted her lips and Camille responded instinctively, slipping her hand behind Issa's neck to hold her closer. The dragon let out a contented hum and deepened their kiss. Camille responded, sitting up straighter in Eben's lap. The kiss had her so tangled up in sensuous abandon she interpreted the caress moving up her inner thigh as being part of it. Eben's low groan hit her ears at the same second fingertips parted her pussy and began stroking.

She gasped against Issa's lips and the dragon-woman pulled away, gazing at her appreciatively. "I may regret letting the Guardian have you both. Perhaps he will share sometimes if you two are amenable." Then with a gust of wind and dragon wings she disappeared again, landing across the room where Geva and Erika were tangled up with each other.

"You liked kissing her," Eben said.

She only nodded, too aroused for words under his soft stroking.

"How long were you out there watching us?" he asked.

"I don't even know." Heat rose up her chest and her face flushed remembering the rush of sensation just before she blacked out.

He nuzzled against her ear. "I want you to stay awake when I make you come. No checking out, alright?" He dipped his head to look into her eyes. She nodded. There was no denying his blue-eyed stare and especially no denying the gentle massaging of his fingers over her clit. Her eyes fluttered closed when one of his fingers ventured deeper, sliding inside the wet heat of her and caressing secret places she'd never been aware of until tonight.

"Camille, you are so tight and wet. I can't wait to feel you ride my cock like you did his. I also can't wait to show you all the other things we can do. Maybe with him. Or even with Issa if you like her as much. Would you like that, baby?"

Camille bit her lip and moaned in pleasure before glancing at Roka. He was attractive, strong and solid, and very, very large. Her pussy clenched around Eben's fingers in reflex when her eyes rested on Roka's still painfully erect cock. She remembered the polished jade shaft she'd deflowered herself on but it was too difficult to reconcile that image with the image of this very alive man. Every bit as alive as the one whose fingertips were giving her so much pleasure at the moment.

She closed her eyes and nodded in response to his question. "Yes, but I want to know what you feel like inside me first." Her words seemed so quiet to her own ears she was worried Eben hadn't heard her at first.

"Mmm…" Eben murmured against her ear. "You have no idea how much I want that. Why don't you turn around so we can give him a show until you're ready for him again?"

Camille let him shift her around so her back rested against his chest and her legs were draped over his. He spread his own legs, forcing hers further apart and slid his hands back down over her breasts and between her thighs. Cool air hit her hot, swollen pussy when he parted her lips for Roka.

"Touch yourself for him, baby," Eben murmured gruffly in her ear.

She gripped one of Eben's arms to steady herself and slipped her other hand down between her legs. Her over-sensitized flesh pulsed under her touch. Eben's strong shoulder behind her caught her head when she tilted it back, sighing under her own caress. She watched Roka from beneath her lowered eyelids, still acutely aware of the press of Eben's cock against her backside.

Roka stood expectantly, a look of blatant hunger in his eyes while his attention focused on her fingers. She slipped them down in an inverted vee, grazing the sides of her clit and squeezing just enough to send a pleasant zing of sensation through her.

Eben's fingertips dug into her hips, urging her to rise.

It was happening now, after all this time. She was going to have him. Maybe it was only a brief taste, but it was a start. She stood, still straddling his hips, her clit throbbing in anticipation.

"Fuck, you have a perfect ass. I could get lost in it."

He gripped each of her ass cheeks in his broad hands and squeezed, spreading her apart. Teasing fingertips trailed gently down the crease, barely brushing the pucker of sensitive flesh. Even that light touch was enough to cause her to gasp in surprise.

"Don't worry, baby, that's for later. Right now I'm on a mission."

He spread her slick, swollen lips with one thumb and forefinger. She heard his breathing quicken when he began to rub the hot tip of his cock against her.

"Does that feel good?" he asked breathlessly.

She realized she'd forgotten to breathe and choked out, "Uh huh."

"Then let me in. All you have to do is …Oh, yeah, just like that. *Fuck*."

She abruptly lowered herself onto him, secretly delighted by the strangled sound he made and the way his fingertips dug painfully into her hips. As new as this was to her, she thought Eben's cock might just be magical. She could *feel* him inside her.

Even the subtle twitch of his hips made her moan in pleasure to feel the head of his cock rubbing some deep, unexplored spot.

Eben laughed. "You like that, baby? I can do that all night."

His hands gripped her ass. With another slow surge of his hips she began to question her sanity.

She raised her eyes back up to look at Roka. The scene felt surreal, even more than her dreams of Eben, and she wondered if she might just wake up after it was all over and find herself back in the jungle, alone in her tent having to listen to the sounds of Eben and Erika going at it mere feet away.

He urged her hips up and down, guiding her on his cock

"Keep touching yourself. Stroke your pretty pussy for him." Eben's low murmur against her ear made her quiver.

Roka's gaze swept up and down her body, lingering on her nipples until they tightened up as though he were touching them. She only became hotter under Roka's gaze when the large man began stalking toward her, his heavy cock bobbing with each step.

He loomed above her, larger than she imagined he could be. She craned her neck to meet his eyes, but they were too busy taking in every inch of her. His scrutiny made her feel suddenly very exposed. More than that, she felt owned by that all-encompassing look of his. The sensation was alien, yet strangely liberating. It was as though no worry would ever be solely her own to bear again because she belonged to him.

Issa's words came back to her then, and for the first time everything clicked into place. *I may regret letting the Guardian have you both*, the dragon-woman had said. That meant Eben belonged to Roka, too. She wasn't sure if she should be so thrilled by the idea, but to be desired by something so magnificent couldn't be a bad thing, could it? And that Roka wanted them both as a couple made her strong desire for Eben seem even more appropriate.

Roka exhaled, emitting tendrils of white smoke that descended down around her shoulders and fell across her breasts in a luminous veil. The soft caress of his breath sent a thrill through every cell it came into contact with.

She sighed and relaxed back against Eben, halting their motions and just enjoying the thick pressure of his cock resting deep within her. His arms moved up to embrace her around her torso, both hands cupping her breasts, raising them up as though they were an offering.

The huge dragon-man knelt before her and flicked his forked tongue out, tickling at her hard, pink nipples. He bent his head lower, as though he were about to lay his cheek against her thigh, but paused. The close proximity of him to the place where she and Eben were joined caused a shiver of anticipatory tension to course through her. What was he doing, poised like that, with his face hovering inches from her? He closed his eyes and his nostrils flared with a deep inhalation. His lips parted and pulled back ever so slightly from pure white teeth as he drew in more air through nose and mouth. She had the distinct impression that he was breathing her in, as if she were some ethereal being he could simply consume that way.

While his head remained bent, she trailed her fingertips along the smooth, curved protrusions of the horns that rested along the contour of his skull. A tremor ran through his muscled torso. Another gust of pale breath fell from his lips like fog and coiled between her thighs. The wispy tendrils made her pussy tingle and she arched into the sensation. Her clit pulsed with need. Eben moaned softly behind her and his hips twitched, pressing his cock deeper into her.

Roka inhaled again, pulling the tendrils of smoke back into him with one long pull of his lungs. The expansion of his chest made him seem even larger. He tilted his head back up and opened his eyes. His pupils were wide and black, but ringed in a circle of speckled silver that glowed.

His low, resonant voice brimmed with lust. "I must have you both. Your mingled scents are too delicious to sample separately. Find your nirvana together, and then you are mine."

He bent his head deeper between her thighs, pressing cool lips against her overheated flesh. His strange tongue slipped out and slicked over her clit, teased and swirled just long enough to leave her poised on the razor's edge of orgasm, then slid down. In a long sweep, he parted her with his tongue, following the length of her wet slit and beyond. A second later Eben moaned behind her. His hips bucked so hard if she hadn't been impaled on his cock, she might have been dislodged from his lap.

Roka gripped her hips to steady her. Then he lifted her, slowly raising her up along Eben's cock. She let him control the rise and fall, following the fascinated roving of his eyes as he watched Eben's cock sink deep into her. Roka raised her up again, his eyes still focused tightly on where they were joined. He bent his head and his long, beautiful tongue went back to work with fervent intent, but she was beyond holding back. With another swipe of his tongue against her throbbing clit, the barrier against her orgasm fell away and she plunged into the abyss.

Eben let out an incoherent cry. After one violent thrust up into her, she felt his climax flood her with pulsing heat. His arms wrapped around her and pulled her back against him tightly while his hips continued moving for a few more strokes.

Her own sweet finale was only just subsiding when she finally opened her eyes to look down. Roka's white hair and majestic horns were all she saw. His tongue still teased alternately between her pussy lips and over the delicate, pink sack of Eben's balls.

Roka stood and reached out a hand to her. It was such an incongruous gesture after what he'd just done she wasn't quite sure how to respond, but after a second she reached up and laid her palm on his. In a swift motion he pulled her to him, wrapped an arm around her waist and lifted her up as though she weighed nothing.

Hot, smooth lips found hers, and his tongue demanded entry. The flavor on him made her moan. Salty-sweet and just a little spicy, like some exotic cocktail. Was that what she and Eben tasted like?

His cock pressed hard against her hip, and with both hands, he lifted her just high enough for it to slip between her legs, the shaft brushing against her still tingling and swollen pussy lips. She wrapped her thighs around his waist, clutching him to her tightly with both arms and legs. The pressure of his cock against her aching flesh reminded her of the intimate moment right before she'd slipped down onto him earlier, but this time he was the one in control. He turned them around and sat beside Eben on the stone altar.

"You know what to do, my love," he growled. "Find your nirvana again on my shaft. Give yourself to me. Prove you are mine and I will prove I am yours."

The buzz from her orgasm had her too dizzy with residual lust, so she only nodded. She braced both hands on his thick shoulders and pressed her hips down. The sensation this time was exquisite and painless, the stretch of her pussy in response to his thickness more like a deep massage that would leave her as pliant as putty afterward. He was only slightly larger than Eben in this form, and with the mix of both her own and Eben's juices saturating her pussy, fucking him now felt like sinking down onto a pole of softest silk.

"That's good," he whispered, white smoke escaping from his mouth and nose with each panting breath. "Now fuck me like you did before."

Her hips knew precisely what to do in spite of a mind muddled with the sensation and the hypnotic scent of whatever magic permeated his strange breath. She gazed into his eyes, lost in their dark pools until he turned away. She followed his eyes to where Eben still sat watching them avidly.

Eben's hand gripped his own cock loosely but he didn't stroke it. When he met Roka's eyes, a spark of desire flashed through his own.

"Give yourself to me again, lover," Roka said. Every syllable he spoke vibrated through Camille, sending trickles of pleasure to her core. "Issa relinquished you, and you gave me your nirvana only a moment ago to seal the bargain, but it will be a sweeter bargain still if I can have both your gifts at the same time I reach my nirvana. It will be an even sweeter gift for the Queen that way, too."

Without a word, Eben moved to kneel on the altar beside Roka and let the larger man pull him into a deep kiss. Watching them both made Camille feel wonderfully lascivious. And so much more so when Roka's free hand reached between Eben's thighs and gripped his thick cock. Eben groaned against the dragon's lips and shifted closer, closing the short distance between them. He raised one foot, resting it flat on the surface of the altar and pressed his other thigh close to hers where it hugged Roka's hip. When Roka released him from the kiss, Eben turned to meet her eyes. His face was flushed and his lips swollen. She accepted his mouth greedily when he bent to kiss her.

At first, she was uncertain how to process the liberation of giving in to both men. She only knew she wanted to do more than be a passive participant. Blindly, she raised her hand the short distance to trace curious fingertips down over Eben's taut stomach. She reached his hips and pulled away from their kiss to watch in fascination as Roka pumped a hand along the length of Eben's cock.

With a hesitant touch, she ran her fingers over the back of Roka's knuckles, feeling his flexing grip. Roka released Eben long enough to urge her small hand around Eben's shaft, then closed his own hand back over hers and squeezed.

"Oh, baby, that's so good," Eben groaned.

She closed her eyes, lost in the steady, deep thrust of Roka's cock inside her and the hot, hard length of Eben's cock pressing against her palm.

Then their touches began. Two velvety tongues teased and nipped at her breasts; lips wrapped around both nipples and sucked. Roka's hand still gripped her hip on one side, so large it nearly covered one ass cheek to guide her up and down on him.

When Eben jerked against her, she knew something had changed and she opened her eyes. His shoulders were hunched, his blond head bent against her shoulder and he let out a series of desperate, incoherent grunts. He seemed to be pressing even further into them both, though the three of them were already so close there wasn't far for him to go.

She saw the reason for his reaction a second later when she spied movement behind Roka. A thick, shape extended along the surface of the altar; the shimmering silvery-white scales resembled the tail he'd had as a statue. It flexed and Eben moaned. She followed the contour of it in a daze. The thick, tapering length of it circled around behind Eben and she realized with a deep thrill of curious arousal that the tip of Roka's tail was now slowly fucking into Eben's ass. And he seemed to like it.

"Oh!" she exclaimed and stared wide-eyed at Roka.

He grinned back at her. "Would it make you fuck me harder if I did it to you, my love? I only have one tail, but perhaps I can improvise for your sake."

If she could have blushed harder, she would have, but he didn't give her a chance to answer. Before she could react, he'd slipped one thick finger of his free hand further between her thighs from behind, soaked it in her flowing juices, and pressed at her tight little asshole. She arched against his chest with a surprised cry, causing Eben to glance up in surprise.

"What is it, baby?" he managed to blurt out. Without answering, she gripped Eben behind the neck and kissed him again, hard and insistent. When Roka's finger passed beyond the sensitive barrier of her anus, she shoved her tongue deep into Eben's mouth. Their moans and pants mingled and they clung to Roka, who set the rhythm. Her pussy clenched hard at the surprising pleasure of the dragon's finger deep in her ass. She'd said she wanted to do dirty things, but wondered if even Eben could have conceived of something quite like this.

Roka's thrusts grew deeper and harsher. Waves of pleasure coursed through her when she met each stroke with a plunge of her hips down onto him.

"Oh, fuck, baby," Eben said. "I love watching you fuck his cock like that. I'm gonna come watching your pussy sliding all over him."

Eben slipped his hand down her back, his fingertips tracing hot fire along the path. His palm cupped and squeezed her ass cheek, then went one step further, teasing a circle around the sensitive skin at the center that was already being slowly penetrated by Roka's finger.

It only took a few caresses and her entire world narrowed into a pinprick of pure pleasure. One pair of lips latched onto her mouth, and another sucked at her nipples again, the sensations coming at her from every direction. A harsh cry erupted from her throat as the tingling throb of climax took hold of her pussy. Her ass clenched tightly around Roka's finger. He plunged it in deep, fucking her with it quickly. Her body seemed to spin out of control. Breathing became almost too difficult.

"Stay with me, my love," Roka's deep voice commanded, his lips brushing against hers. "I'm close."

She was dimly aware of the air shifting around them and the thick weight of Roka's cock growing even larger inside her. Nothing else existed of her body but the coiling mass of sensations that held her lower body captive. The dragon's cock surged into her at the same time Eben let out a long, low groan against her shoulder. The room grew darker as their bodies shuddered and writhed together. Something hot and wet splashed against her stomach. More hot liquid covered her hand where it gripped Eben's cock within the confines of Roka's larger hand.

Roka's low roar escalated around them. It pulsed against her eardrums, extending the sensations higher, so that her skull seemed to resonate with the same pleasure that gripped her body and made her nipples tingle. With another deep, violent thrust, wet, scorching heat filled her pussy.

Instead of the darkness of blacking out, the world became a thick, white fog.

She clung desperately to the two figures, not quite sure now where she ended and they began. The aftershocks of her orgasm gradually subsided, but only after the long, steady pulses of Roka's cock finally ceased inside her.

Finally she let out a long, shaky breath and collapsed against his chest, resting one cheek against him. Eben sat back on his heels, head bowed, sweat-soaked blond hair obscuring his face. His glistening cock rested limp against one thigh.

She looked beyond him but could see nothing but the fog and realized they were cocooned inside Roka's wings. The pair of massive white membranes almost completely encompassed the three of them, embracing them within a chamber filled with the dragon's breath. She inhaled deeply, taking it into her lungs. The more she breathed, the more the tension of their encounter dissipated, leaving her relaxed and euphoric. And still conscious.

"I didn't pass out," she said, smiling at no one in particular.

Roka rumbled softly. His gentle touch skimmed down her spine. "No. My magic prevented it this time. I needed you conscious."

"So you're awake for good now?" she asked, looking into his eyes. His pupils were now narrow slits surrounded by silver irises that gleamed with inner light.

"Yes. And now you both are mine. A dream come true for a dragon to be so blessed upon first awakening. You must help me thank Issa once the ritual is complete. There is one more thing I must do, however."

He shifted her off his lap and urged her to lie flat. Curious, and eager to please, she did so, uncertain what was coming next. He bent over her hips and his tongue flicked out, tracing a small design just above the golden curls of her pubic hair.

She winced at the sting, but it dissipated quickly once he blew on it with a quick puff of white fog.

He turned to Eben. "Your turn."

Eben met Camille's eyes and shrugged. "It's a pretty tattoo. White, too—you can barely tell it's there unless you were looking for it." He obligingly lay down for Roka and received his own mark.

Camille stared down at the slightly upraised circular mark. Upside-down it didn't look like much, but she could make out the shape of a tiny dragon in embossed white. She wondered if Erika had been given one, too.

At that moment, the lights around the room flared brightly, then dimmed again. She and Eben both glanced around in surprise. She noticed Erika sit up on the other side of the room, attentive to the disturbance.

Propelled into action, Kris began walking toward the door, but none of the dragons made a move to follow.

"What was that?" Eben asked.

"Someone has opened the second door," Roka said. "The next phase has begun. Soon the Twins will be awakened."

ABOUT OPHELIA BELL

Ophelia Bell loves a good bad-boy and especially strong women in her stories. Women who aren't apologetic about enjoying sex and bad boys who don't mind being with a woman who's in charge, at least on the surface, because pretty much anything goes in the bedroom.

Ophelia grew up on a rural farm in North Carolina and now lives in Los Angeles with her own tattooed bad-boy husband and four attention-whoring cats.

You can contact her at any of the following locations:
Website: http://opheliabell.com/
Facebook: https://www.facebook.com/OpheliaDragons
Twitter: @OpheliaDragons
Goodreads: https://www.goodreads.com/OpheliaBell

Printed in Great Britain
by Amazon